WELCOME TO THE NEIGHBORHOOD

WELCOME TO THE NEIGHBORHOOD

Debbie Bloy

To order additional copies of this book, contact:
Xlibris
1-888-795-4274
www.Xlibris.com
Orders@Xlibris.com
778806

WELCOME TO THE NEIGHBORHOOD

BY DEBBIE BLOY
WITH STEVE STERN

ILLUSTRATED BY DIETRICH SMITH

CHAPTER ONE

Debbie looked at the check that had just been handed to her by the president of the Foodstuff Corporation. She knew in advance how much it was going to be made out for, but it still made her eyes bulge.

"You look surprised," the man, whose name was Harold Wentworth, said.

"I think I'll just sit down for a minute," Debbie said, settling into an overstuffed chair.

"Don't spend it all in one place," Mr. Wentworth said with a little laugh.

"I don't think I could," Debbie told him.

And she was certainly right. Debbie had spent several years in the restaurant business in Scottsdale, Arizona, opening one successful restaurant after another. And now she'd sold all four of them to the Foodstuff Corporation for what her father would have called "a pretty penny."

"What are you going to do now?" Mr. Wentworth asked her.

"That's easy." Debbie smiled. "I'm going to get a dog."

A few days later, Debbie's brand-new gleaming white Rolls-Royce pulled up in front of a modest home in Buckeye, Arizona. Inside the house lived Gertrude Potts and a dozen or so bichon frises. Debbie had always wanted a bichon, and Ms. Potts ran a highly recommended bichon frise rescue.

As soon as Debbie entered the house, lots of little white furballs were scampering and yipping around her feet. They were all so cute! Debbie wondered how she was going to pick out her perfect animal companion. What she didn't suspect in the least was that one of the pups was actually going to pick *her*!

That's exactly what happened. A small female bichon fixed her gaze on Debbie and thought, *What a beautiful lady. I have to get her to pick me.*

Many of the other dogs were already scampering around Debbie, so the little female had to think fast. She backed up to the other side of the room then took a running leap and jumped over all the other pups straight at Debbie, who had no choice but to open her arms and catch her.

The little bichon took that opportunity to lick Debbie's chin and look lovingly into her blue eyes.

"What a little darling," Debbie commented to Mrs. Potts.

"Oh yes. She's a cutie."

Debbie was about to say "I'll take her" when another pup stood up on his hind feet and started dancing in front of Debbie. He was just as cute as the bichon Debbie was holding, who happened to be his sister. The only difference between them was that the male dog was several pounds heavier, so his little tummy was sticking out a bit.

"Oh no," he thought. "She probably thinks I'm too chubby! Now she'll never pick me."

To his surprise, Debbie knelt down and gave him a big grin. "Aren't you a talented little man," she commented.

Still holding the little female, Debbie picked up her brother and gave him a kiss on the nose.

"Oh no," thought his sister. "She's going to pick *him*."

Debbie was talking to Mrs. Potts. "They're both so cute, I don't know which one to pick," she admitted.

"Why don't you take both of them?"

"That's a great idea!" Debbie said, squeezing the pups to her. "That way, they'll always have company. And we'll be a real family."

"I like the way she thinks," the female said to her brother. Of course, to humans, it sounded like she was just barking—but that's how dogs communicate, the same way people talk to each other.

"What are you going to name them?" Gertrude asked Debbie.

It didn't take very long for Debbie to answer. "I think I'll I'll call them Neiman and Marcus, after my favorite department store."

CHAPTER TWO

Debbie had grown up in Canada and had always been fascinated with America—more specifically, Beverly Hills. As far as she was concerned, Beverly Hills was the most glamorous place on earth. She had dreamed of moving there ever since she was a little girl, and her dream got one step closer to becoming true after she graduated from college. But instead of going directly to Beverly Hills, Debbie moved to Scottsdale, Arizona, where her aunt and uncle had gone to live several years earlier.

Debbie started her career working in a restaurant, and within two years, she found herself opening her own eating establishment, with a small loan from her parents. A year later, she opened her second restaurant, followed by a third and a fourth. Each restaurant was more successful than the one before it. And then one day, Debbie was approached by the Foodstuff Corporation, which owned restaurants all over the country. They wanted to add all her establishments to their chain.

As soon as she decided to take their very generous offer, Debbie was determined to move to Beverly Hills and achieve her ultimate childhood dream. What she didn't know was that the little female bichon she had just named

Neiman had the same dream—and then some. Neiman didn't just want to move to Beverly Hills; she wanted to become a famous actress, like Lassie and the other big canine stars.

As the chauffeur drove smoothly across the highway, Debbie sat in the back seat of the Rolls, playing with her new pups.

"You two are certainly very talkative," Debbie told them, noticing how much barking and yipping and yapping was going on. Of course, what she didn't know was that Neiman and Marcus were engaged in a meaningful conversation.

"This is so amazing," Neiman told her brother. "You know I've always wanted to get to Hollywood—and that's exactly where we're headed."

"Oh please," Marcus said, shrugging his fluffy shoulders. "The next thing I know, you'll be telling me that it's all part of some master plan."

"It is!" Neiman said emphatically. "It's clear that I'm destined to become the most famous actress of all time!"

"Spare me," Marcus drawled. "Acting, in a word, is gauche."

"There you go again with your huffy attitude," Neiman shot back. "You're just jealous."

"I am not!"

"Oh really? I saw how you reacted when Debbie picked me up. You just had to make sure that she chose you too."

"Well," Marcus said, "that's different. I was only looking out for your welfare."

"*My* welfare?"

"Precisely. I mean, someone had to come along to keep you out of mischief. I am, after all, your older brother."

"You're also my *chubby* brother." Neiman snorted.

"I'll have you know I happen to like my shape," Marcus huffed. "And obviously, Debbie does too."

They went on like that for quite a while until the chauffeur looked into the back seat and said, "We'll be arriving at our destination in about an hour, ma'am."

"I can't wait!" Debbie said excitedly. Then she turned to the dogs and added, "I'm going to have to look for a home to buy. But until I find it, I've got a real treat in store for all of us."

"I wonder . . . what could it be?" Marcus asked his sister.

And then Debbie answered his question. "We're going to be staying at one of the most fabulous hotels anywhere—the Beverly Hills Hotel!"

CHAPTER THREE

Debbie stepped out of the Rolls-Royce in front of the Beverly Hills Hotel with Neiman and Marcus in their deluxe carrying bag. She walked up the red carpet. It was just like the red carpet Debbie had seen at the Academy Awards on TV, complete with a photo backdrop for taking pictures. But this backdrop said, "Take a STEP back in time AND REPEAT Hollywood's Golden Age." And below that, it said, "The Beverly Hills Hotel and Bungalows." In front of the backdrop was a thick red velvet rope that VIPs would step behind to have their picture taken.

Debbie thought, *Neiman and Marcus are VIPs—very important pooches*. She placed the carrying bag behind the rope then zipped it open so they could stick their heads out. Debbie stepped back a few feet and started snapping pictures with her phone.

"We're already stars," Neiman said to her brother.

"Oh, come on," he said. "We just got here. And besides, I have no intention of becoming famous. I like my life just the way it is."

"Don't be such a fuddy-duddy," his sister told him. "We're at one of the most famous spots in the world, so enjoy it. Besides, I *am* going to become a movie star."

Marcus knew better than to argue with his strong-willed sister, so he just decided to smile and humor her.

Debbie picked up the bag, saying, "You two are certainly chatty today. Now be nice and quiet while we check in."

Neiman and Marcus did as requested, and before long, they were being led to their bungalow by a very nice concierge named Betty, followed by a bellboy who rolled a cart with all of Debbie's suitcases on it.

"Welcome to the Pink Palace," Betty said. "We hope you'll enjoy your stay with us as much as we'll enjoy having you here."

Marcus thought, *Why do they call it the Pink—?* And then he stopped himself when he looked around and saw that all the walls were pink.

Betty pointed to one of the bungalows as they walked past it. "Bungalow number 7 here was one of two bungalows that Marilyn Monroe liked to stay in. The other was bungalow number 1, which is the most private and secluded bungalow we have."

Debbie had to pinch herself to make sure she wasn't dreaming—because making it all the way from Canada to Beverly Hills had been her lifelong dream, and now that dream had become a reality. Years and years of hard work, plus a little luck along the way, had led up to this day.

Betty turned the key in the door to Debbie's bungalow, which opened to a magnificent living room with a fireplace that had a gold-framed mirror above it, a luxurious couch, and chairs sitting on a multicolored Persian rug. There was also an entertainment center that included a large flat-screen TV.

"I love it," Neiman told her brother as she jumped out of the carrying bag and hopped right up on the couch.

"I hope it's okay that she's on the couch," Debbie said as the bellboy unloaded the bags.

"Of course it's okay," Betty told her. "When we say that the Beverly Hills Hotel is dog-friendly, we mean it!" Betty had been carrying a large canvas bag that she now reached into. "In fact, we have a very special gift for both Neiman and Marcus."

Marcus had already joined his sister on the couch as Betty pulled the first of two dog bowls out of the bag. But these weren't just any dog bowls. They were pink ceramic bowls that said *Beverly Hills Hotel and Bungalows* on the front, and the hotel's distinctive crest could be found at the bottom of each bowl.

"Look at the wonderful present you've been given," Debbie told the bichons.

Neiman and Marcus stood up on the couch and licked Betty's hands in thanks as she placed the bowls next to them.

"I've got something else to show you," Betty said, leading the three of them into the bedroom, which was dominated by a magnificent four-poster bed.

"How luxurious!" Debbie commented.

"And these are no less luxurious," Betty said, pointing at the two plush pink doggy beds that sat in a corner of the room.

Neiman and Marcus hopped right onto them and made themselves comfortable.

"I never want to leave here," Neiman said.

"Well, we will be leaving," Marcus reminded her, "once Mom finds our house." They had heard Debbie talking on the phone to the realtor, who would be coming to meet her tomorrow so they could start the process of house-hunting.

"Just let us know if you need anything else," Betty said as she and the bellboy left the bungalow a few moments later.

Debbie placed the bowls next to the doggy beds, opened a bottle of water that was on the coffee table, and poured water into each of the bowls. Neiman and Marcus lapped the water right up.

"You two were thirsty," Debbie said, twisting open another bottle. "Come to think of it," she said, drinking, "I'm thirsty too."

Five minutes later, Debbie and her Beverly Hills bichons were fast asleep in their beds, all of them dreaming about the wonderful things to come.

CHAPTER FOUR

The next morning, Debbie and the pups got up early and took a stroll through the winding pathway that connected all the bungalows. When they got back, Debbie ordered room service, and they had breakfast on the patio overlooking their private garden. Debbie had eggs Benedict, and the pups ate their special blend of dog food—which Debbie had brought along—out of their pink bowls.

"Now I've got another special treat for you," Debbie told Neiman and Marcus as she changed into her bathing suit. "I've reserved a poolside cabana for us."

Neiman was so excited she started dancing around and yipping away, telling Marcus, "How exciting! I know we're going to meet lots of special people at poolside. Maybe even some celebrities!"

Marcus started yipping too. "Stop being so starstruck. It's positively uncouth."

"Uncouth?" Neiman shot back. "Why don't you just use your favorite word, *gauche*?"

"Why? Because I have an extensive vocabulary, and I enjoy using it."

"Well, then I've got one new word for you—POOH!" snapped Neiman.

They were still sniping back and forth at each other as Debbie, wearing the fluffy white Beverly Hills Hotel bathrobe that she found hanging in the bathroom, placed their carrying bag on a chaise lounge in the gorgeous poolside cabana. On the rear wall was the same deep green banana-leaf wallpaper that lined the hotel's hallways.

"I'm going to take a dip in the pool," Debbie said, taking off the bathrobe. Neiman and Marcus jumped out of their bag and made themselves comfortable on the chaise. They watched as Debbie stuck her toe into the pool and then dove in.

"Why don't we take a swim?" Neiman asked her brother.

"You're kidding me, right?" Marcus replied. "Dogs aren't allowed in the pool."

"That's just silly." His sister pouted.

"Don't worry," Marcus consoled her. "Mom has promised to buy us a house with a swimming pool, and we'll be able to play in it anytime we want."

Debbie stayed in the pool longer than she intended to—the water was just the right temperature, and she also met some of the other guests who were taking an early afternoon swim. Everyone seemed very nice.

"That was fun," Debbie told her pups as she toweled herself off a half hour later. As if she could read their minds, she added, "Soon, you'll have your own swimming pool."

After a while, a white-clad waitress from the poolside restaurant came over, introduced herself as Kelly, and handed Debbie a menu, saying she'd come back in a little while to see if Debbie would like to order lunch. Debbie liked eating salads for lunch, and sure enough, there were several on the menu. The first one listed was the McCarthy Salad, which Debbie had never heard of. But from its ingredients, it seemed similar to a salad Debbie was very familiar with—a Cobb salad.

When Kelly came back, Debbie asked, "Why do you call it a McCarthy Salad?"

Kelly laughed. "Lots of people ask us that! Neal McCarthy was a well-known polo player who ate here all the time. He liked Cobb salads but preferred that they were chopped up, so everything got mixed together. Our chefs were happy to do that for him and eventually named the salad for him. It became our most popular salad and still is."

"In that case," Debbie said, "I'll have to try it."

The salad came with a bread basket, as well as something else. Kelly also presented Neiman and Marcus with two complimentary dog biscuits. "These are made with chicken liver, bacon, chicken broth, cornmeal, and flour, and topped with a ketchup glaze," she said. "They're a specialty for our canine guests."

Neiman and Marcus eagerly took the biscuits from the waitress's hands and started eating. They found the biscuits to be as tasty as any treat they'd ever had, and Debbie thought the McCarthy Salad was nothing short of sensational. In all her years in the restaurant business, she had never heard of the McCarthy Salad—which only went to prove that you could always learn new things.

When they went back to the bungalow after lunch, Debbie turned on the television, and they watched CNN for a half hour, catching up on the news. Debbie was a big believer in always being informed about what was going on in the world.

"I'm going to take a shower now," she told the pups afterward, "and then our real estate agent is coming over to meet me."

"That's great," Neiman barked. "The sooner we get our own swimming pool, the better."

An hour later, Debbie walked into the Polo Lounge, where her new real estate agent, Janet, was waiting for her at the bar. Debbie was outfitted in her signature white designer tee-shirt and jeans with rips in them, while Janet was dressed in a very professional-looking tailored pantsuit. They gave each other a hug, took a table, and ordered drinks.

"You're a lot younger than I thought you were," Debbie told her.

"So are you." Janet laughed.

Debbie laughed too. "I can see we're going to get along famously."

"Since you only arrived yesterday," Janet said, "is this your first visit to the Polo Lounge?"

Debbie said it was, and Janet asked her if she knew the history of the Polo Lounge bar. When Debbie shook her head, Janet pointed at the large photo on the wall, directly behind the bar.

"You see those two polo players? I'll tell you who they are in a moment. But first, the reason it's called the Polo Lounge is that, back in the day, the man who managed the hotel had a friend who was a national polo champ. When his friend asked if he could display the team's trophy—a silver bowl—in the hotel, the manager agreed to display it right here in the bar. And from that day on, this became the Polo Lounge."

"And those two polo players in the picture?" Debbie asked.

"One of them is the actor Will Rogers, and the other is film producer and studio executive Darryl F. Zanuck. They both loved to play polo and hung out here all the time."

Debbie was impressed. Darryl F. Zanuck was the legendary producer of some of Debbie's favorite classic films, including *All About Eve*, *The Grapes of Wrath*, and *How Green Was My Valley*.

Their drinks were delivered, and the two women clinked glasses. "Here's to finding the house of your dreams," Janet toasted.

CHAPTER FIVE

For the next few weeks, Debbie followed the same routine every day. She'd get up in the early morning hours, walk Neiman and Marcus on the pathway between the bungalows, and feed them in their pink bowls. Then she would work out in the fitness center, have a massage in the spa, and by noon, eat a late breakfast in the Fountain Coffee Room. After that, she'd play with her pups in the garden, then get dressed and wait for Janet to pick her up for another round of house-hunting. That would go on until about six o'clock, at which time Janet would take Debbie back to the hotel. Then it would be time for another walk with the pups and then their dinner, after which Debbie would have her own dinner in the Polo Lounge.

Each night, Debbie would review the list that Janet would email her of homes that had just come on the market that day, or were about to come on the market, and there were always plenty of fabulous houses to look at. But none of them seemed to be exactly what Debbie was looking for. *I'll know it when I see it,* she assured herself.

One day, Janet picked her up looking more excited than usual. "Today just might be your lucky day." Janet grinned as Debbie got into her cream-colored Jaguar.

"Oh really?" Debbie said. "And why is that?"

"Well, our agency has just been given the exclusive on a very special property." And she handed Debbie a listing sheet that described the house she was referring to. There was also a picture included, of a large white Mediterranean-style home.

"Looks nice," Debbie said.

"We're heading right over there before anyone else sees it," Janet informed her, stepping on the gas. "It's only five minutes from here."

Debbie read through the listing on their way over. It was a six-bedroom home with four and a half baths, which was larger than Debbie needed, but she certainly didn't mind taking a look at it. "You said it's a very special property," she said to Janet. "What makes it so special?"

"I'll let *you* be the judge of that," Janet said with a little wink.

Within minutes, they were pulling up in front of the house. Debbie followed Janet up the slate walkway to the front door. Janet unlocked the door, and they went inside.

The house was empty; all the furniture had been removed. Debbie was struck by how spacious it was.

Janet pointed to the large room off to the right, saying, "Look at this magnificent step-down living room. It has wood-trussed ceilings, a fireplace, and beveled glass wood-framed windows."

"Gorgeous," Debbie said.

For the next hour, Janet led Debbie through all the rooms, which included a kitchen with a marble-topped island in the middle, a formal dining room capable of sitting at least twenty people, a family room, butler's pantry and den, plus the six bedrooms on the second floor. The master bedroom included a large balcony that overlooked the backyard.

They went back downstairs, and Janet led Debbie out a set of french doors into the yard, which was dominated by a blue-tiled swimming pool that—as far as Debbie was concerned—rivaled the pool at the Beverly Hills Hotel. Also in the back of the house was a three-car garage. "There's even a bonus room inside the garage," Janet said.

Debbie had to catch her breath. "I love it," she breathed. "I can see why you said it's so special."

Janet smiled. "You think so, huh?"

Debbie didn't know what she was getting at. "I don't understand . . ."

Janet kept smiling. "Remember when we met in the Polo Lounge and I showed you the picture behind the bar?"

"Of course."

"Do you remember who was in that picture?"

"Of course. Will Rogers and Darryl F. Zanuck."

Janet nodded. "And didn't you tell me that Darryl F. Zanuck was one of your all-time favorite movie producers?"

"I did."

"So," Janet said, still grinning, "how would you like to live in Darryl F. Zanuck's home?"

Debbie's jaw dropped open. "You mean—?"

"Yes, this was the home of one of Hollywood's most famous movie moguls. And it's yours if you want it."

Debbie felt as if she was going to faint. *I'll know it when I see it*, she reminded herself.

"I want it!" she said. "This is my new home. And I know Neiman and Marcus will love it too!"

CHAPTER SIX

Over the following weeks, Debbie made plans for what she wanted to do with her new home. She met with contractors, interior designers, and landscapers, all of whom began working as soon as the paperwork was finalized.

Debbie would drive over to the property in her Rolls-Royce every day to deal with the people she had hired. She wanted to get everything done as soon as possible. One day, when she went over to meet the pool man, her new neighbor came outside to greet her.

"I'm Goldie," the woman said. "Goldie Fishman. Welcome to the neighborhood." Goldie was several years older than Debbie, with gray hair that was pulled back into a bun. She was carrying a small box with a ribbon around it.

"Here's a little present for you, just something that I baked myself."

"That's so nice," Debbie said, taking the box.

"That's a lovely car you have," Goldie said, nodding toward the Rolls-Royce.

"Thank you. I've only had it for a couple of months."

Goldie squinted at the license plate. "I see you have Arizona plates."

"Yes," Debbie said. "I've been living in Arizona."

"But you're not American, are you?" Goldie said, pursing her lips. "I can hear the slightest accent."

"Very observant," Debbie said, forcing a little smile. "I'm Canadian."

"So what brings you here to Beverly Hills?"

The questions went on and on. *Talk about a nosy neighbor*, Debbie thought. After a few more minutes, the pool man came driving up, and Debbie was relieved to be able to tell Goldie that she had to go.

Dave the Pool Guy—that's what it said on the side of his van—got out of the vehicle along with a red-headed teenage boy.

"This is my son, Justin," Dave told Debbie. "He's helping me out this summer, learning the business."

"It's a pleasure to meet both of you," Debbie said, watching Goldie leave. "Believe me, it's a real pleasure."

They went into her house, and Debbie took them out to the pool, which was covered with a tarp. Debbie pulled the ribbon and opened the box that Goldie had given her. Inside were some small cookies with a dab of something that looked like jelly in the middle.

"Do you like cookies?" Debbie asked Dave and Justin. She held the box out to them, and they each took a cookie. Debbie tried one of them. It was too sweet for her taste. She handed Justin the box. "Enjoy!"

Debbie went back inside the house as Dave and Justin went about pulling the tarp off the pool. A few minutes later, her cell phone rang. It was Debbie's older brother, Wayne.

"How's it going, sis?" he said. "When do you move into the new place?"

"Any day now," Debbie said.

"That's great! How'd you like to have a houseguest starting next month, eh?"

Canadians often ended their sentences with "eh"—something that Debbie had taught herself to keep to a minimum since moving to America.

"You want to come visit?"

"I'm talking about Lois," Wayne said, referring to his daughter.

Lois was Debbie's favorite niece, and Debbie was Lois's favorite aunt.

"I'd love to have her!" Debbie exclaimed.

"That's great, sis. Gemma and I are finally going to take that two-month cruise of the South Pacific. Lois can stay with Randy [that was Debbie's younger brother], but she said she'd love to spend the time with you. And for the month of August, we're going to book her into the Beverly Hills Sleepaway Camp."

"Beverly Hills Sleepaway Camp, eh?" When Debbie was talking to a fellow Canadian, the "ehs" had a habit of slipping right back into her speech pattern. "It's perfect that she'll be there in the month of August, because that's when I'm going out of town for Doris's wedding."

Doris was one of Debbie's closest friends from Scottsdale, and she was finally getting married.

"It'll be a real experience for her," Wayne said, and they went on to discuss the details of Lois's visit. Debbie was excited to have Lois as the first guest in her new home.

"Wait till she meets Neiman and Marcus," she said enthusiastically.

"You mean the department store people? Sounds like you're really moving up in society there."

Debbie laughed. "Oh, that's right. I haven't told you, eh? I've got a pair of lovely bichon frises now, a brother and sister."

"Let me guess," Wayne said. "Neiman's the girl, and Marcus is the boy, eh?"

CHAPTER SEVEN

"Welcome to your new home!" Debbie said a few days later as she lifted Neiman and Marcus's carrying bag out of the Rolls.

"Yes, welcome," called out a voice.

Debbie turned to see Goldie trotting over from her yard.

"What cute little puppies!" Goldie said.

"Who's that?" Neiman asked her brother as they both stuck their heads out of the top of the bag.

"That's obviously the 'nosy neighbor' Mamma told us about," Marcus drawled.

Goldie patted their heads. "They don't bite, do they?"

"Of course not." Debbie laughed. "Neiman and Marcus, meet Goldie."

"I love those names," Goldie said, continuing to pet them.

"Get us away from her," Marcus said.

Debbie apparently understood because she told Goldie that she had to go inside, to get ready to interview candidates to be her new housekeeper.

Debbie opened the front door and placed the carrying bag on the floor, and the pups jumped excitedly out of it.

"Just look at our beautiful new home," Neiman barked out.

"It's positively glorious!" Marcus marveled. "I love the furniture!"

The day before, the movers had delivered Debbie's new furniture. The place was really shaping up. Debbie looked outside to see that the gardeners had arrived to work on the landscaping.

Neiman and Marcus ran all over the house, checking out one room after another. Upstairs in the master bedroom, they found their pink Beverly Hills Hotel beds that Debbie had purchased for them.

"I'm going to love it here!" Neiman said, jumping onto her bed.

"What's not to love?" Marcus agreed.

Soon, Debbie was busy interviewing housekeepers. By late afternoon, she had seen a half dozen candidates, all of whom were very well-qualified and came with impeccable recommendations. The last interview of the day was with a man named Frank DeMois. He arrived precisely on time for his four o'clock appointment.

"Come right in," Debbie said, opening the door for him.

"Thank you, mum," he said with what sounded to Debbie to be a British accent. Frank DeMois was very trim and had a shaved head. He was wearing a tailored pinstripe suit with a crisp white shirt and bow tie.

"It says on your résumé that you're Australian," Debbie said as they sat in the living room, "but your accent sounds British."

"Well, mum, I'm originally from Australia, but I spent several years in Great Britain. And I must say, those were some of the best years of my life."

"I'm Canadian myself," Debbie told him.

"Jolly good!" Frank replied. "I've never met a Canadian I didn't like."

"Is that so?"

"Absolutely, mum."

Marcus came walking by at that moment and caught sight of Frank. He liked what he saw, so he padded over and sat beside Frank's polished shoes.

Frank reached down and patted Marcus's head. "And who's this lovely fellow?"

"That's Marcus," Debbie told him. "And his sister is Neiman."

"Neiman and Marcus—I love it."

Marcus immediately knew that he wanted Debbie to hire Frank, so to get his point across, he went over to her and started nodding his head furiously up and down. "Don't let this fellow get away, Mamma."

"It's obvious that Marcus likes you," Debbie said.

"I can assure Master Marcus that the feeling is mutual."

Debbie reviewed Frank's résumé with him and was impressed with all his qualifications. She gave him a tour of the house, including the housekeeper's quarters, and Marcus followed them from room to room. When they arrived in the master bedroom, where Neiman was lounging on her bed, Marcus told his sister, "This is Frank, and he's going to be our new housekeeper."

Frank bent down and patted Neiman on the head. "Pleased to make your acquaintance, Ms. Neiman. I daresay you're cute as a button."

"Oh yes," Neiman told her brother. "He's a keeper." She jumped up and started licking Frank's face.

Debbie had already made up her mind. "They both really like you," she told Frank. "Guess what? You're hired!"

CHAPTER EIGHT

When Debbie woke up the following morning after sleeping in her new house for the first time, Neiman and Marcus were cuddled up beside her, having left their own beds during the night to join her. Golden sunlight was streaming in from the balcony, and everything was as Beverly Hills–perfect as Debbie had always dreamt it to be.

"Good morning, pups," she beamed, squeezing them to her.

"And good morning to all of you," said Frank as he entered the room carrying a tray. On it were three decaffeinated coffees. Debbie's was in a mug, and Neiman's and Marcus's were in cup-shaped bowls with their names inscribed on them.

Frank, wearing a crisp white apron, placed the bowls next to the doggy beds. "You're certain it's all right for them to drink coffee, mum?" he asked Debbie.

"As long as it's decaf, it's absolutely fine," Debbie said. "But no cream, as dogs are lactose intolerant." They had discussed the subject last night, after Frank had returned with his belongings, since he was available to start work immediately.

"I trust m'lady slept well," Frank said, placing her mug on the nightstand.

"I slept like a baby," Debbie said.

"Your copy of *Variety* arrived, along with the *LA Times*." Frank handed them over. "Are you in, as they say, 'the business'?" he asked.

"Oh no," Debbie said. "But since I'm living here, I thought I might as well be in the know."

"Absolutely." Frank nodded. "Hollywood is fascinating, and you're right in the middle of it here. I believe that most, if not all, of the big talent agencies are located in Beverly Hills."

"Did you hear that?" Neiman asked her brother as they lapped up their decaf. "I told you. I'm going to become a star. A dog star."

"You mean you're Sirius, in the constellation Canis Major," Marcus said dryly. "Commonly referred to as the dog star."

"There you go again, trying to be clever. You know exactly what I mean," Neiman huffed. "There's plenty of work for 'Canis Majors' in the movies."

"Dream on, sister."

"You'll see," Neiman barked, shaking her tail in his face. With that, she jumped up on the bed, where Debbie was reading the *LA Times*. The copy of *Variety* was sitting next to her, and Neiman started pawing through it.

"Brilliant," Frank said, watching her as he was leaving the room. "If I didn't know any better, I'd say she was reading."

Debbie laughed. "What makes you think she isn't? My pups are very special."

Neiman was, in fact, reading—and her attention was galvanized when she got to page 6. At the bottom of the page was a small article entitled "Remake of *It's a Dog's*

Life Set for Next Year." The article stated that the remake of the classic 1955 film (about a dog who braves the mean streets of New York's Bowery district, only to become the toast of the city when he wins several prestigious dog shows) would be casting roles for several dogs.

"Look at this! Look at this!" Neiman told her brother, who hopped up on the bed.

"What's got you so excited?" Marcus asked.

Neiman pointed to the article and told him to read it.

"You can't think they'd actually hire you," Marcus said after he'd done so. "You have no acting experience, and this is a big-budget film."

"I've got natural talent," Neiman protested. "All I need is a chance."

"Don't be silly, little sister."

"I'm not being silly!" Neiman insisted. "Besides, Mamma would love for me to be a star." She turned to Debbie. "Isn't that right, Mamma?"

Debbie looked at the clock on the nightstand and bolted out of bed. "Look how late it is! My personal trainer will be arriving any minute!"

"Oh pooh!" Neiman huffed. "No one's listening to me!"

Debbie ran into the bathroom to get ready for her new Pilates trainer, who would be coming to the house three days a week.

"Just be satisfied with what you've got," Marcus told his sister. "And what we've got is a lot."

"I'm not saying we don't," Neiman countered, "but that doesn't mean I can't dream big." She jumped off the bed and trotted down the stairs, telling herself, *I'm going to become a movie star, one way or another!*

CHAPTER NINE

That evening, after dinner, Neiman trotted out the open french doors that led to the pool. She padded her way to the front gate and looked out onto the street through the wrought iron bars.

"What are you doing out here?" Marcus called from behind her.

Neiman turned to look at him and made a face. "There you go again—following me everywhere."

"Well, someone has to look out for you," her brother commented. The next thing he knew, Neiman had slipped out between two of the bars. "Hey! You can't do that!"

"I just did," Neiman replied.

Marcus rushed up to the bars and stuck his nose out through them. "Just what do you think you're doing, young lady?"

"If you must know, I'm going to find myself an agent. That's the only way I'm going to get to audition for that movie—and become a star!"

That was all Marcus could take. "Get back here!" he ordered, advancing on the fence. But . . . he couldn't get through the bars.

"Ha ha!" laughed Neiman. "You're too chubby to make it through."

"And you're too obstinate for your own good," Marcus said, still trying to squirm between the bars. "Get back here this instant, or I'll tell Mamma."

"Don't you dare," Neiman warned. "I'll be just fine. I'm just going to take a stroll down the block."

"What good is that going to do you?" Marcus barked with exasperation.

"This is Beverly Hills," Neiman explained. "I'm sure there are agents living in lots of these houses."

"But it's dark out," Marcus pleaded. "It could be dangerous."

She kept moving down the street. "Oh, stop being such a scaredy-cat—I mean, dog."

"Don't—"

"Just relax. I'll be back soon," she said, already past Goldie's house.

What Neiman didn't know was that two sets of eyes were already on her. Fortunately though, they were eyes belonging to two do-gooders. More specifically, they were the identical eyes of two twins. The Chin Twins—Tom and Don—were, in fact, animal control officers for the City of Beverly Hills. They weren't on duty, however, as their normal hours were from nine to five. After the sun went down, they became something quite different—wannabe Beverly Hills cops. Ever since moving into the 90210 zip code three years before, Tom and Don had wanted to be police officers. They gave it their best shot, but their bodies were too out of shape to pass the physical exam, and their minds were a few IQ points too low to pass the written test. So they settled on being animal control officers; but they patrolled the streets of Beverly Hills by night, seeking out crime.

"That looks like a bichon frise," Tom said. "What's it doing walking alone at night?"

"It's either lost," Don said, "or it's up to no good."

"Either way," Tom chimed in, "that dog is under our jurisdiction."

"Yeah. Let's go get it."

They were about a block away from Neiman when they spotted her, and they were about half a block away from her when she spotted *them*.

"Uh-oh," Neiman told herself and took off at a run.

The Chin Twins followed suit. "She's on to us," Tom breathed. Just walking fast had raised a sweat on his brow. Now he and Don started running.

"Stop! Stop!" yelled Don between labored breaths. "By the order of the Animal Control Unit."

Neiman was having none of it. She dashed across the front lawn of the house on the corner, then zigzagged across the backyard and onto the grounds of the adjoining house, coming out on the next block over.

Omigod, Neiman thought, *Marcus was right. I never should have gone out alone.* She heard the labored breathing and heavy footfalls of the two strangers who were still chasing her and calling out, "Stop, you furry little criminal!"

Neiman looked around wildly and spotted a low hedge in front of the house across the street. As her pursuers rounded the corner, she sprinted across the road and then bounded over the hedge.

They'll never catch me now, Neiman thought triumphantly as she ran through the yard and out onto the next street.

A split second later, she was bathed in a blinding white light as a large car screeched to a halt only inches away from her.

CHAPTER TEN

Artie Silver jammed on the brakes of his silver Mercedes-Benz and gasped. *Oh man*, he thought, *I almost hit that little dog!*

Artie opened his door and stuck his head out. "Are you okay, puppy?"

Neiman was frozen in the headlights. She was standing directly in front of his license plate, which read #1 AGENT.

"Are you okay?" Artie asked. "You must be lost."

He's an agent! Neiman thought, unfreezing herself. *Not only that, but he's the number 1 agent!* She pranced around to the side of the car, and before Artie knew it, she'd leapt into his lap.

Artie was relieved to see that she was wearing a collar that had a phone number inscribed on it. He closed the door and drove off just as the Chin Twins huffed and puffed themselves into view.

"Don't worry," Artie told Neiman. "I'll get you right back to your owner." He tapped his Bluetooth and told his phone to dial the number on her collar. When Debbie answered, he said he had a cute little bichon frise in his car.

"What!" Debbie nearly screamed. She was watching TV on the couch, with Marcus sitting on the floor next to her. When she asked Marcus where his sister was, he promptly got up and ran out of the room.

Artie explained how he found Neiman wandering the streets. He didn't want to alarm her owner by explaining how close their encounter had actually been and said he'd be happy to bring her directly home. Debbie gave him her address. She was waiting anxiously at the door when Artie drove up two minutes later. He was carrying Neiman and handed her over to Debbie.

"What happened?" Debbie asked Neiman, who simply shrugged her furry little shoulders. On the one hand, Neiman was ashamed about the incident; on the other, she was excited to have found herself an agent.

Marcus came scampering up and asked his sister the same question. Her answer: "Just wait and see!" With that, she ran up the stairs.

Debbie asked Artie to come in so she could properly thank him for saving her dog. By the time they sat down on the sofa, Neiman had returned—with the copy of *Variety* in her mouth. She jumped up on the couch between Debbie and Artie and pawed through the tabloid until she came to page 6.

"What were you up to, out on the street?" Debbie asked her.

Instead of answering, Neiman started pointing to the article about *It's a Dog's Life*.

"Now that's a savvy little puppy," Artie said. "She reads the trades." He laughed.

"Are you in the entertainment industry?" Debbie asked.

"Well, I don't want to blow my own horn—or maybe I do," Artie said, grinning, "but I'm the top agent at CIA."

Debbie blinked. "You-you're a spy?"

Artie laughed again. "Oh no, not *that* CIA. I'm a talent agent at Creative International Agency. C-I-A."

Marcus was stunned. "I absolutely do not believe this."

"Believe it," Neiman said. "I told you I was going to find an agent."

Debbie wagged her finger at Neiman. "Don't ever go out to the street by yourself again."

Neiman kept jabbing her paw into *Variety* until Artie spied the article. "Wait a minute," he said. "She's trying to tell us something."

He picked up the tabloid and read the article out loud. Then he said, "I get it. She wants to audition for a part in the movie."

I do not believe this, Marcus thought.

"I always knew Neiman was smart," Debbie said, "but this really takes the cake."

"So," Artie asked, "would you like to give her a shot at the big time?"

"Are you serious? How would I even do that?"

"Simple," Artie said. "I sign on as her agent and get her into the casting call. It's not as if she needs years of acting lessons. Besides, she looks like a natural to me. Some of the biggest actors in the world never had a lick of train—" He suddenly stopped and bent over with laughter.

"What's so funny?" Debbie said.

"I said 'a *lick* of training,'" Artie said when he caught his breath. "That's what dogs do—they lick things, right? Man, I crack myself up. Ha ha ha!"

Neiman leapt into Artie's lap for a second time that evening and started (what else?) licking his chin.

Artie took out a silver-plated business card case and handed Debbie his card as he rose to leave. "Call me tomorrow, and we'll get the paperwork done."

He turned back to Neiman and held out his hand. Neiman raised her paw and Artie shook it.

"This looks like the start of a beautiful friendship," he said in his best Bogart imitation.

CHAPTER ELEVEN

When Frank brought in the morning coffee, Debbie told him about all the excitement he'd missed last night after he'd fallen asleep.

"It sounds like you had quite an adventure, Ms. Neiman," he told her as he placed her bowl in front of her.

"You don't know the half of it," Marcus commented.

"How do you think she got out on the street?" Frank asked Debbie.

"She must've just walked out through the gate," Debbie said. "She's certainly tiny enough to get through."

Frank looked concerned. "How can we prevent that from happening again?"

"Oh, I think I've taken care of that. I told her the streets are off-limits, unless she's on a leash."

"You told her?" Frank said.

"Absolutely. You have no idea how intelligent she is."

"I'm not doubting that for a moment. And you say this little trip yielded her a top Hollywood agent?"

"I know. It sounds unbelievable."

"Unbelievable," Marcus echoed.

"Don't be jealous," Neiman said. "Be happy for me."

"And she's also going to be auditioning for a role in a big-budget film," Frank marveled.

"Exactly. She pointed out the article in *Variety* to us."

"Brilliant!" Frank said. "Ms. Neiman is, without doubt, the most intelligent member of the canine species that I've ever encountered."

"Did you hear that?" Neiman asked her brother.

Marcus lowered his head, shaking it back and forth. "Unbelievable," he said again then padded out of the bedroom.

Two hours later, Debbie was at Los Angeles International Airport, waiting for Lois's flight to arrive. Debbie hadn't seen Lois in almost a year and wondered how much she had grown. As Lois came down the escalator leading to the baggage-claim area, Debbie could see that the answer was a lot. Lois had transformed from a girl into a young lady.

They hugged for a long time, telling each other how wonderful they looked. "But you're a bit overdressed for Los Angeles," Debbie said. Lois was wearing a knit wool cap, a ski jacket, and corduroy pants. "It's eighty-five degrees here today," Debbie informed her.

"It was about thirty degrees cooler back home," Lois said. "But I feel fine."

They retrieved her bags and wheeled them out to Debbie's Rolls.

"This is your car, eh?" Lois stared at it, her mouth agape. "I've never been in a Rolls-Royce before. Heck, I've never even *seen* one—except in a magazine."

Lois and her family lived on the outskirts of the city, and Debbie knew that she was an outdoorsy type of girl who spent most of her spare time doing things like playing sports and hiking in the woods. There was going to be a certain amount of culture shock—especially when Lois saw the house she'd be staying in.

On the ride back to Beverly Hills, Lois talked nonstop about school, her friends, the soccer team she was on, and her favorite cause: saving the environment. "We've got to protect our forests and endangered species, like the polar bear," she said with conviction. "When I go to university, I want to study environmental science."

"That's wonderful," Debbie said as she took the Santa Monica Boulevard exit off the highway. "I'm very proud of the young lady you've become." Soon they were driving past a large cluster of tall office buildings.

"Is that Beverly Hills?" Lois asked.

"It's Century City," Debbie explained. "Many of the big movie and TV companies have their offices here."

"I don't know too much about that," Lois said. "I don't spend very much time watching TV or going to the movies."

Debbie turned off of Santa Monica Boulevard onto her street. She pulled to a stop in front of her home.

Lois stared at it for several seconds. "Wow. Who lives in that mansion? I'll bet it's some movie star, eh?"

If Neiman has anything to say about it, Debbie thought, *a movie star will be living in there.* What she said to Lois was "Not really. That's my house."

Lois's jaw fell open again. "You-you're kidding, right?"

Debbie's answer was to open her door and get out of the car. "C'mon, let's go inside and meet the family."

Lois didn't move for several seconds. Then she opened her door and said, "Uh, I'll get my bags."

"No need. Frank, my housekeeper, will get them."

Lois stopped in her tracks. "You have a *house*keeper?"

"I see you've got a lot to learn about the Beverly Hills lifestyle," Debbie said.

"That's for sure," Lois said, following her through the security gate. She shrugged her shoulders. "We don't even have a wooden fence around our house."

Frank opened the front door for them, saying, "Welcome, Ms. Lois."

Debbie introduced Lois to Frank as Neiman and Marcus ran out to greet her. Lois knelt down and hugged each of them.

"Neiman's the little girl, and Marcus is her big brother," Debbie said. "Say hi to Lois, kids."

"I can see the familial resemblance," Marcus said.

"So can I," Neiman agreed, "except she looks like she's dressed for an expedition to the North Pole. This girl is going to need a makeover."

CHAPTER TWELVE

After helping her unpack in the guest room, Debbie gave Lois a tour of her home. "This is the biggest house I've ever been in," Lois remarked.

"Me too." Debbie laughed. "But it's far from the biggest house on the block. Would you like to see the neighborhood? We can take Neiman and Marcus for a walk."

"Sure, why not?" Lois said.

They put the pups on leashes and headed out.

Goldie Fishman opened her door as they walked in front of her house. "Hi there!" she called, walking outside in her housecoat.

"Hi, Goldie." Debbie waved.

"Here she comes," Marcus drawled. "That insufferable woman will have a million questions for us."

"And who do we have here?" Goldie asked, coming up to them.

"This is my niece Lois," Debbie said, introducing her to Goldie.

"And where are you from, dear?" Goldie asked.

"A small town in Canada," Lois replied.

"So you're visiting your aunt. How long will you be here?"
"For about three months. But the last month, I'll be going to the Beverly Hills Sleepaway Camp."

"Oh, that sounds lovely. Have you been to Beverly Hills before?"

"No, this is my first time."

"And how old are you?"

"Thirteen."

And the questions went on and on until Neiman and Marcus started pulling. Debbie was relieved to say that the dogs needed to move along and do their business.

"Come over and visit some time," Goldie said as they left.

"I'm sure we will," Debbie said, which was the last thing she wanted to do.

They passed by several other houses on the block, each one larger than the one before it. Gardeners were working in many of the yards.

"Everything's so big here, and so perfect-looking," Lois remarked.

"That's true," Debbie said.

"Dad said that even as a little girl, you knew you wanted to live here someday."

"Yes, I was always fascinated with Beverly Hills."

"It certainly is different, eh?" Lois said.

They went another block then crossed the street and walked back on the other side. As they passed one of the homes, two kids of around Lois's age came out, walking a corgi.

"Hi!" Neiman called out to the corgi. "My name's Neiman. What's yours?"

"I'm Bramwell," the corgi said. "And who's that handsome guy with you?"

"That's my brother, Marcus."

"Hi, Marcus," Bramwell said, coming up to sniff his nose.

"Nice to meet you, Bramwell," Marcus said politely.

Debbie smiled at the girl who was walking Bramwell. "I'm Debbie. What's your name?"

"I'm Nancy," the girl said, "and this is my brother, Lawrence."

"Larry," her brother said. "I like to be called Larry."

Lois introduced herself, and then Nancy pointed at her wool cap. "What's that?"

"It's called a toque," Lois said. "Everyone in Canada wears a toque."

Nancy made a face. "Then it must be freezing in Canada, because you don't need to wear one here."

"The same goes for the ski jacket and those heavy slacks," Larry said. "They're not very stylish either."

Debbie thought the kids were being very rude, but she kept a smile on her face and said, "This is Lois's first trip here. We'll be getting her some new clothes tomorrow."

Lois made a face. "We will, eh?"

"Sure, why not? We'll go shopping on Rodeo Drive."

"Then make sure you go to the Rodeo Drive Boutique for kids," Nancy suggested. "That's where I got this cool outfit."

"That must cost a lot, eh?" Lois said.

Nancy shrugged. "I just put it on my credit card."

"You say 'eh' a lot, don't you?" Larry smirked.

"It's a Canadian thing," Lois said.

"Well, now you're in Beverly Hills," Nancy said.

"We'd better get going now," Debbie said to the kids. "See you around the neighborhood."

When they were out of earshot, Debbie said quietly to Lois, "They're a bit snooty, aren't they?"

"For sure. None of my friends back home are like that."

"They just need to get to know you," Debbie said.

"I wonder if all the kids at the sleepaway camp are going to be like that."

Debbie wondered the same thing.

CHAPTER THIRTEEN

Neiman's audition for a part in *It's a Dog's Life* was fast approaching. Debbie suggested to Lois that they take Neiman and Marcus to the Pampered Pooch Beauty Salon on Rodeo Drive, after which they could buy Lois some new clothes.

"I really don't want any new clothes," Lois said, "but the Pampered Pooch sounds like fun."

Debbie didn't want to pressure Lois, who obviously had a mind of her own, so off they went to the salon. When they arrived, several dogs were being groomed, and they were told that there would be about an hour's wait before Neiman and Marcus could be taken.

"That's fine," Debbie said. "We'll just walk around town."

Debbie pointed out several of the well-known stores: Gucci, Prada, Versace, Louis Vuitton, Giorgio Armani, Chanel, and Dior, among many others.

"I just love it here," Neiman told her brother.

"What's not to love?" Marcus replied.

"I've never seen so many designer names in one place," Lois remarked.

"That's why this is one of the world's most famous streets. People come here from all over to shop."

"I hope they bring plenty of money," Lois said.

After they'd walked for a while, Debbie spotted an ice cream shop on a side street, and they took one of the tables in front of it. Debbie took the portable bowl and bottle of water that she always had with her and gave the pups a drink. Lois went into the shop and bought ice cream—chocolate for her and vanilla for Debbie. As they were eating, a white stretch limo stopped across the street, and a man and a woman wearing baseball caps and big sunglasses stepped out and went quickly into one of the stores.

"They must be someone famous, eh?" Lois said.

"No doubt. I've seen lots of movie stars here," Debbie explained. "Also lots of international jet-setter types." As she was looking across the street, Debbie noticed that one of the smaller storefronts was empty and had a FOR LEASE sign in the window. She took out her phone and snapped a picture.

"What?" Lois asked. "Are you trying to get a shot of those people so you can figure out who they are?"

"Actually, I'm interested in that empty store," Debbie said, pointing it out.

"Why? Are you thinking of opening another restaurant?"

Debbie shrugged her shoulders. "I wasn't actually thinking of it, but I'm always looking for new opportunities." In fact, she was already formulating an idea.

It was late afternoon when they returned to the house. Both Neiman and Marcus looked fabulous, having been trimmed, bathed, and blow-dried. Each pup was adorned with a ribbon—pink for Neiman and blue for Marcus.

Lois wanted to take a dip in the pool and went upstairs to change. Debbie said she had some business to take care of and called Janet, her real estate agent. When Lois came downstairs in her bathing suit, Debbie was getting ready to leave again.

"I'll be back shortly," she said. "Have fun in the pool."

"You certainly are having a busy day," Frank, who was preparing dinner, said to Debbie.

"Yes, I like to keep busy," Debbie said, closing the door behind her.

"You have quite an amazing aunt there," Frank told Lois.

"For sure. Dad said his sis was always coming up with one business idea or another. And look how successful she's become."

"Indeed. And what about you?" Frank asked. "What are you interested in doing?"

"I want to be an environmental scientist," Lois said brightly. "We've got to protect the Earth for future generations."

"That's very laudable," Frank said. As Lois headed out to the pool, he asked if she would like anything special for dinner.

"Do you know how to make butter tarts?"

"Butter tarts?"

"They're the best," Lois said. "Everyone in Canada eats butter tarts for dessert."

"I'll look up the recipe," Frank said as Lois headed to the pool.

While Lois was swimming, Debbie was meeting Janet at the empty storefront she'd seen. Janet had already arranged to get the key, and they went inside.

"It's a small space, but very elegant," Janet said, looking about. "It's been sitting vacant for a while."

Debbie walked around for several minutes. "Hmm. Hmm. Hmm."

"That's a lot of *hmm*ing," Janet said. "What are you thinking?"

"I'm thinking of something groundbreaking for Beverly Hills," Debbie suddenly said.

"What?"

Debbie didn't answer for a moment. Then she said, "If I tell you, you'll have to swear to secrecy."

"Of course." Janet held out her pinkie. "Pinkie swear."

Debbie held out her pinkie, and they crossed fingers.

Then Debbie told Janet her idea, to which Janet exclaimed, "You're a genius!"

CHAPTER FOURTEEN

It was the day of Neiman's audition for *It's a Dog's Life*, which was held in the Beverly Hills offices of the producer of the film. When Debbie arrived with Neiman and Marcus in their carrying bag, there were already several other dogs and their owners in the reception area. Also in attendance were Tom and Don Chin, who greeted everyone at the door.

"We're the animal control officers," Tom announced. "We like to do everything by the book here in Beverly Hills."

Don added, "When it comes to your four-legged friends, we're *their* best friend—as well as yours."

It had been quite dark on the night that the Chin Twins had spotted Neiman walking by herself on the street, so they didn't recognize her; nor did she recognize them. It was as if they were all meeting for the first time.

A production assistant with a clipboard in hand approached Debbie and asked for the names of her dogs. "Neiman and Marcus," Debbie said, "but only Neiman is auditioning. She and her brother are inseparable."

The production assistant checked off Neiman's name on the clipboard and nodded. "Of course. Please have a seat."

Debbie took a chair next to a woman in a bright red pantsuit who had a string of large pearls dangling from her neck. Sitting on her lap was a miniature poodle. The woman introduced herself to Debbie as Margot Legrand. She spoke with a French accent.

"Bonjour," Debbie said.

"Are you French?" Madame Legrand asked.

"No. But I grew up in Canada, so I have many French friends."

"*Magnifique.* I see you have bichons."

"Yes." Debbie pointed them out. "This is Neiman, and this is Marcus."

Madame Legrand laughed. "Neiman and Marcus! How very cute!"

"Your poodle is just as cute," Debbie said. "What's her name?"

"Zis is Star Legrand. My fabulous little actress."

Upon hearing that, the miniature poodle struck a pose, holding her head high and pursing her lips.

"Wow, that's very dramatic," Neiman told her.

"Thank you," Star Legrand said, also with a French accent. "I am a true thespian."

"I'm new to the acting business," Neiman admitted, "but I'm a fast learner."

"I see," Star Legrand said, although she sounded far from convinced.

The production assistant tapped her pencil on the clipboard and said, "Okay, everybody, we're going to get started with the auditions now. You'll go inside one at a time as I call your names."

Tom Chin went up to the production assistant and said, "I'll stay here, and my brother will stay in the audition room. That way, we have everything covered, and there'll be no shenanigans."

"Shenanigans?" the production assistant said.

"You know, so that everything stays aboveboard."

The production assistant shrugged her shoulders. She knew she had to go along with the local authorities—even if, in this case, they were a pair of overachieving twin brothers. "Whatever," she said.

But someone *was* up to no good at that very moment. When Debbie turned her head for a few seconds, Madame Legrand opened her hand in front of Neiman's nose. In her palm was an innocent-looking dog treat, and it smelled wonderful to Neiman. She gobbled it right up.

"What was that?" Marcus said. Madame Legrand had moved so quickly, Marcus had barely caught a glimpse of what had happened.

"The nice lady gave me a treat," Neiman said. "She obviously likes me."

"That's your problem," Marcus said. "You think everyone likes you."

"If you were more sociable, everyone would like you too."

"I prefer to be more discerning," Marcus huffed.

The first dog's name was called, and her owner led her into the audition room. Madame Legrand took out a business card and handed it to Debbie.

"As you have bichons, you may be interested in my services," Madame Legrand said.

Debbie looked at the card:

CHATEAU BARKLEY
Boarding for Non-Shedding Dogs
MARGOT LEGRAND
Owner

"What a unique concept," Debbie said.

"Thank you. When I see an opportunity, I take advantage of it. Owners of non-shedding dogs do not want them associating with dogs who do shed."

As each auditioning dog finished and left the office, the next one went in. Soon the production assistant called for Star Legrand.

There were only a few dogs and their owners left when Madame Legrand and Star exited the office.

"We'll be going in very soon," Debbie told her pups.

Neiman was feeling overheated. "It must be my nerves," she told her brother.

"Perhaps you have stage fright—without the stage," Marcus joked.

"Not funny," Neiman said. *Maybe my nerves are getting the best of me*, she thought, realizing that she was panting.

Finally, her name was called. Debbie carried the pups into the audition room. Two people were sitting at a table toward the back of the room, and there was a chair to sit in opposite the table. The production assistant stood behind a video camera that was mounted on a tripod. Don Chin stood stiffly in a corner, watching everything that was going on with a serious expression on his face.

"I'm Donald Lawson," one of the men at the table said, "the producer of this film."

"And I'm Lawrence Fitzgerald, the writer," the other man said. He wore a brightly colored plaid jacket and a paisley ascot.

What an interesting-looking man, Marcus thought.

"I see we have two lovely bichons here," said Lawrence.

"Yes, but only Neiman is auditioning. Marcus came along to be her cheering section."

"Neiman and Marcus—I love it! Why don't you take Neiman out of the bag and place her near the *X*."

Two pieces of gray tape on the floor marked an *X*.

Neiman's feet were wobbly as Debbie put her on the floor. In addition to sweating and panting, she was also feeling dizzy. She had a strange taste in her mouth, and she remembered that she had eaten the treat Madame Legrand had given her.

"I-I'm not feeling well," she told her brother.

"What's the matter?" Marcus called out.

To the humans in the room, of course, it simply sounded like the dogs were barking at each other.

"Do they always act like that?" the producer asked.

"Not always," Debbie said. "You two hush up," she told her pups.

"Let's try running through a scene," Lawrence said, motioning to the production assistant to start taping. Lawrence stood up and gestured with his hands, waving them up and down. "Okay, Neiman, let's see you jump up and down, like you're happy to see your owner come home."

Neiman understood what he wanted and tried her best to jump up, but her legs gave out under her, and she fell on her face.

"This will never do," the producer said.

Neiman struggled to stand up and almost did, but then her legs went out again, and she crashed to the floor.

Don Chin came running over, saying, "Everyone out of the way. I'm a professional. Let me see what's wrong with her." He knelt down and put his face an inch away from Neiman's.

"Her eyes are dilated," he said. "This definitely isn't normal."

"Of course it's not normal," Debbie said, pushing him away as she scooped Neiman up and put her back in the carrying bag. "She obviously needs to rest and have some water."

"Yes, that's a good idea," Don Chin said. "Give her some water."

"I thank you for coming," the producer said, "but we have to move on."

"Wait!" Lawrence suddenly said, eyeing Marcus. "Would you mind if Marcus auditioned? I have a small part that I think he'd be perfect for."

CHAPTER FIFTEEN

Neiman was beside herself as they returned home. Fortunately, the effects of the treat that Madame Legrand had given her had worn off. But that didn't make her feel any better about what had just happened.

"She must have drugged me with that treat," she told Marcus as they jumped out of the carrying bag and ran upstairs.

"You can't be certain," her brother told her. "It may have just been nerves. Or maybe it just didn't agree with you."

"Why should *you* care?" Neiman snapped as she jumped into her bed. "That writer even gave you a bit part."

"I can't help it if he liked me," Marcus said evenly. "And I wouldn't exactly call it a *bit* part. I mean, I don't *bite* anybody."

Neiman didn't bother laughing at Marcus's attempt at a joke. "Madame Legrand wanted to make sure I didn't pass the audition so her precious Star would have a better chance of getting the part."

Marcus got into his bed beside her. "Even if that was the case, how would we prove it?"

Lois looked in on them as she passed the door to Debbie's bedroom. She then continued downstairs, where Debbie was talking to Frank, who was putting a pan in the oven.

"How'd it go?" Lois asked.

Debbie shook her head sadly. "Not well. I was just telling Frank. Neiman got an attack of nerves or something and couldn't perform."

"Oh, that's terrible."

"I thought I was going to have to take her to the vet. But fortunately, she recovered quickly."

"Has something like that ever happened before?" Frank asked.

"No, except she never had to audition for a part before. She's very high-strung, so who knows? At least she seems fine now."

"I'm so sorry for her," Lois said. "I'll take her for a nice long walk later, if she's up to it."

The bell rang, and Frank answered the door. Artie Silver waved at Debbie as he stepped inside.

"This is my niece Lois," Debbie said. "Artie is Neiman's agent."

"That's right," Artie said, shaking Lois's hand. "I never had a dog for a client before. There's a first time for everything. Anyway, I was on my way home and thought I'd stop by and see how the audition went."

"I'm afraid it didn't go so well," Debbie said sadly. She explained what had happened.

"That's terrible," Artie said. "But I'm glad to hear she's feeling better now."

"I guess it's not all bad news," Debbie said. "Marcus actually got a small part in the film."

"Marcus?"

"Yes. The writer liked him and said he'd be perfect for a minor role."

"That's fantastic!" Artie said enthusiastically. "I'll write up a representation agreement for him and drop it off tomorrow."

"Will he have to sign it?" Lois asked. "You know, like with a paw print?"

Artie was heading to the door. "Good question, but no. Debbie's his legal guardian, so she'll sign it, same as she did for Neiman." He opened the door. "That's the crazy thing about Hollywood," he said. "You never know who's going to become a star. Gotta run!"

Debbie sniffed at the air. "What's that smell?" she asked Frank. "Are you baking something?"

Frank checked his watch. "They should be ready now." He put on an oven mitt and took the pan out of the oven. "Voila! Butter tarts!"

"You made them!" Lois said with delight.

"Of course. You said you wanted them."

"I haven't had butter tarts in longer than I can remember," Debbie said, picking one up carefully. It was still piping hot. She took a small bite.

Lois did likewise. "Delicious!"

"Don't spoil your appetites, ladies," Frank cautioned. "Dinner will be served in ten minutes."

After dinner, the girls took Neiman and Marcus for a walk. The sun was starting to go down, so Lois pulled on her toque and ski jacket. Neiman was back to her old self, walking briskly at the end of her leash. Debbie was relieved.

"I'm sure there'll be other acting opportunities for Neiman," Debbie said.

Neiman scowled at her brother. "There better be!"

"I'm sure Mamma's right," Marcus told her.

"And don't let the fact that you've got a role in that movie go to your head."

"Believe me, I won't."

They turned at the first corner and headed toward the next block. "Dad told me you'll be going to your friend's wedding while I'm at camp," Lois said.

"Yes, in Arizona. But that will just be for a few days."

"I hope I like camp," Lois said.

"I'm sure it'll be fun."

Up ahead, Nancy and Larry were walking Bramwell. When they caught up to them, Nancy said, "I see you're still wearing that—what did you call it?—tope."

"Toque," Lois said.

"And that ski jacket," Larry said. "Didn't you go to the boutique we told you about?"

"We, uh, haven't gotten around to it yet," Debbie said, trying to be diplomatic.

Neiman went up to Bramwell and said, "What's with those kids? They're so rude."

"Tell me about it," Bramwell said. "I've been living with these two brats since I was a puppy."

"Too bad you can't teach them some manners," Marcus commented.

CHAPTER SIXTEEN

The next morning, Lois was sitting outside, reading a thick book entitled *How to Save the Earth*, when Dave and Justin arrived to do the weekly maintenance on the pool. Lois introduced herself to them.

"You're from Canada," Dave said.

"That's right."

"Then you're going to be as cool a person as your aunt. I already told her that I've never met a Canadian I didn't like."

"That's nice to hear." Lois smiled.

Dave started cleaning the surface of the pool for leaves and debris with a skimming net. "Why don't you take a break and talk to Lois?" he told his son. "It's not every day you get to talk to a bona fide Canadian."

Justin sat on the chaise lounge next to hers and asked, "How long will you be here?"

Lois closed her book. "Well, I'll be staying at the house for a few more weeks, and then I'll be spending the month of August at the Beverly Hills Sleepaway Camp."

"Wow. That sounds pretty neat."

Lois shook her head. "I'm not so sure."

"What do you mean?"

"Well . . ." She hesitated. "Do you live in this neighborhood?"

"No. We live in the Valley."

"What valley is that?" Lois asked.

"The San Fernando Valley. You've heard of 'Valley girls,' haven't you?"

"Oh, right," Lois said. "They say things like 'that's totally rad' and 'eww, that's grody.'"

Justin laughed. "That's a pretty good imitation. Some of the girls in my class sound just like that. So why did you ask if I lived in this neighborhood?"

Lois shrugged. "Well, to be perfectly honest, some of the kids around here seem very stuck-up to me."

Justin looked at her seriously. "No. You're kidding, right?" And then he burst out laughing.

Lois laughed too. "So you know what I'm talking about."

"Like, I totally do," Justin said, and they both laughed again. Then he added, "I'll bet you met Nancy and Larry from across the street. We take care of their pool too."

"Seriously, why do you think they're like that?" Lois asked.

"It's really pretty obvious," Justin said. "A lot of the kids around here—I'm not saying all of them—get everything they want. So some of them are going to be snobs. Did you ever see that show *The Real Housewives of Beverly Hills*?"

"No, but I've heard of it."

"All you have to do is watch an episode, and you'll know exactly what I mean."

"I think I already do," Lois said.

Justin pointed at Lois's book. "I see you're concerned about the environment."

Lois nodded enthusiastically. "I want to become an environmental scientist."

"That's great," Justin said, getting up. "I guess I'd better help my dad clean up the environment right here."

"Nice meeting you," Lois said.

Justin stopped and looked back at her. "Don't worry about those other kids at the sleepaway camp," he said, "and don't ever change."

Lois smiled to herself and reopened her book.

While Lois was talking with Justin, Debbie was over at the storefront she'd just leased in downtown Beverly Hills. Workers were delivering a large commercial oven. Debbie showed them where it would be hooked up in the kitchen area.

"So what's this gonna be," asked one of the workers, "the trendiest new bistro in town?"

"That's top secret," Debbie said.

"I know," said another worker. "It's gonna be some kinda fusion restaurant—like Japanese-Italian or Mexican-Chinese."

"Keep guessing," Debbie teased.

A third worker laughed. "German-Argentinian."

"Hawaiian-Armenian."

"Greek-Bolivian."

"You've just given me ideas for five new restaurants." Debbie grinned. "But you're not even close."

Debbie had designed all her restaurants in Scottsdale, and this place would be no exception. She had a pad in hand and was sketching out what the dining area would look like. This would be the smallest eatery she'd ever owned, but it would also be the most exclusive. She hadn't really thought about getting back in the business after selling her restaurants to the Foodstuff Corporation, but when the idea hit her, she knew she had no choice. She could already envision lines around the block, waiting to get in.

CHAPTER SEVENTEEN

"So what is your new restaurant going to be like?" Lois asked Debbie one morning.

Debbie told her.

"What a great idea," Lois said. "You're so talented, Aunt Debbie. Look at how much you've already achieved."

"We all have something we excel at," Debbie said, sipping decaf coffee. "You're going to be a great environmentalist, helping preserve our world for future generations. What you'll be doing is very important."

"I certainly hope so."

They were having breakfast together on Debbie's balcony. It was a beautiful morning, without a cloud in the sky—which meant it wasn't very different from most every morning in Southern California.

Lois had already been at Debbie's for over a month, and every day was as warm and sunny as the next. "Does it ever rain here?" she asked.

"That's a good question," Debbie said.

Lois took out her cell phone and typed "average rainfall in Beverly Hills" into her browser. "Not very much," she said a few seconds later, reading the information on the screen. "The average rainfall here is about half the national average. And even less than half of what we get back home. That's why you have to be concerned about drought here."

"You see?" Debbie said. "You're already talking like an environmentalist."

After Lois went off to play with the pups, Frank came out onto the balcony to collect the breakfast dishes. Debbie noticed that he was looking very pale.

"Is something the matter?" she asked.

"I'm afraid so, ma'am. I just received a most distressing phone call. My mother is quite ill."

"I'm so sorry to hear that. Does she live in Australia?"

"Yes. She's now in her early nineties."

"Then you must go see her," Debbie said firmly.

"I don't see how—"

"I'll pay your month's salary in advance," Debbie said. "That's not a problem."

"That's truly most kind of you, ma'am. But you have Ms. Lois here, and you'll be attending your friend's wedding next week."

Debbie thought about it then said, "Lois starts sleepaway camp in a few days, so she won't even be here. And I know just where to board Neiman and Marcus."

"Are you certain?" Frank said, placing plates on a tray.

"Absolutely. Now go make your reservations."

Debbie went inside and dug into her handbag, where she found the business card that Madame Legrand had given her. She called the number on the card, and a moment later, Legrand herself answered.

"We met at the audition," Debbie reminded her. "I'd like to board Neiman and Marcus at Chateau Barkley."

"Of course. I'll come to your home, and we'll make the arrangements."

"Why don't I just come to your place of business?"

"I provide a very exclusive service," Legrand said. "Now give me your address."

* * *

When Madame Legrand clicked off her phone, she turned to Morty Craven—the short, heavyset man she called her "business partner" but who was, in fact, her partner in crime. As was Star Legrand.

"We got us anudda mark," Legrand chortled in an accent that sounded more like Brooklyn than Paris. Which made sense since she was born in Brooklyn.

Madame Legrand's real name was Trixie Kane, and Star Legrand's real name was Sophie Smith. Years back, when they were both still in New York, Trixie found Sophie wandering the street with a pack of wild dogs. The two of them bonded immediately, and along with Morty, they came up with a master plan: they would go west and open a dog-boarding business in Beverly Hills, one of the wealthiest communities in the nation, and use it to rob the well-heeled residents there.

And now Trixie had found her newest "mark"—Debbie!

* * *

Two hours later, "Madame Legrand" showed up at Debbie's house. "What a lovely home," she said, sounding French again.

When they heard the bell ring, Neiman and Marcus ran from their beds—where they were relaxing—to the top of the stairs, to see who had arrived.

"I can't believe it! It's the woman who poisoned me!" Neiman barked out.

Legrand looked up and eyed the pups, saying, "Oh, there are those two darling bichons."

"Grrrr," Neiman said.

"Be nice now," Marcus said. "We don't know for sure if she did anything of the sort."

"This house is so fabulous," Legrand told Debbie, putting her plan into effect. "Would you mind giving me a quick tour?"

Legrand knew that Debbie wouldn't refuse, and she followed her throughout the house. Legrand had her phone in her hand, and when they passed by the keypad for the house's alarm system, she snapped a picture of it with her camera.

When they sat down in the living room at the end of the tour, Legrand said, "Have you heard? My precious Star has been selected as the female lead in the film."

"Congratulations to the both of you," Debbie said. And she added, "But don't let Neiman hear that. She's very sensitive."

But Neiman, standing right outside the room, had already heard. She ran back upstairs to tell her brother the infuriating news.

"I hate that woman," she growled, "and I hate her mangy mutt!"

CHAPTER EIGHTEEN

Debbie and Lois dropped Frank off at the airport the next morning, and a few days after that, Debbie was dropping Lois off in front of the posh Beverly Hills Sleepaway Camp. It was located on a very private street in the "Hills" section of town. True to form, Lois was wearing her toque and ski jacket despite the warm weather.

"Are you sure you want to be dressed like that?" Debbie asked as Lois got out of the Rolls.

"I'm fine," Lois said.

"Okay then, see you in a month. Have fun." Debbie watched as Lois made her way toward the front gate, where several other kids were assembled. They all stared at her as she approached. Debbie thought, *She reminds me of me.* Then she drove away.

When she got home, Debbie started packing for her trip to Doris's wedding. She'd met Doris shortly after arriving in Scottsdale, and they had become the best of friends. Debbie would be away for a week, which would also give her time to catch up with some of her other friends in the area.

That night, as they all got in bed together, Debbie told Neiman and Marcus that they'd be staying at Chateau Barkley for a week.

"She thinks we don't already know," Neiman told her brother. "I really don't want to go there. It's going to be gross and disgusting."

"Oh, come on now. We might even make some new friends." Marcus always liked to look on the bright side of things.

"I hope Star Legrand won't be there." Neiman smirked. "She'll be so full of herself."

"Don't be jealous now, just because she got the lead role."

"She only got it because her owner drugged me!" Neiman protested.

Debbie was watching them bark at each other. "What's gotten into the two of you?"

"She should only know," Neiman said.

* * *

Sure enough, when Debbie dropped the pups off at Chateau Barkley the next morning, Star Legrand (a.k.a. Sophie Smith) was waiting at the door beside Margot Legrand (a.k.a. Trixie Kane).

"Welcome to the Chateau Barkley," Legrand cooed in her false French accent. "I guarantee that Neiman and Marcus are going to have a wonderful time here."

"I'll bet," Neiman said, sneering at the miniature poodle.

"Welcome to our humble abode," Star said.

"Don't play the innocent game with me," Neiman snapped.

"Please don't take what my sister says seriously," Marcus interrupted. "She hasn't been quite herself since the audition."

"I heard you also got a part," Star said.

"Yes, but let's not discuss that right now. I don't want to aggravate Neiman any further than she already is."

Soon, Debbie was saying goodbye to her pups. "I'll see you in a week," she said, giving them both a big hug.

"If we survive it," Neiman said.

"Stop being so silly," Marcus said. "And try to enjoy yourself. We have some new friends to meet."

He was right. There were three other dogs being boarded: a wheaten terrier named Max, a greyhound named Lulu, and a miniature schnauzer named Fritzie.

Morty Craven came out from the back after Debbie had left and introduced himself to Neiman and Marcus. "Hiya, pooches. I'm Morty, your new best friend."

"You're not *my* friend," Neiman barked.

"Can't you at least be sociable?" Marcus asked her.

"Puh-leese," Neiman said.

"You've got to get your sister under control," Star told Marcus.

"Easier said than done."

All the dogs were in the common play area. Fritzie came up and said, "I'm with Neiman. That Morty is a creep."

"He is not!" Star protested, although she knew better.

Lulu ran up with a ball in her mouth and let it drop to the floor. "Let's all play and have some fun," she said. "I'm not into drama."

"That's too bad," Marcus joked, "because my sister is a drama queen."

"Very funny," Neiman said, kicking him.

Max picked up the ball in his mouth and threw it in the air. "Catch!"

Fritzie jumped up and grabbed the ball, and soon everyone was playing together. Even Neiman was beginning to enjoy herself. Although, of course, she wouldn't admit it.

* * *

Two nights later, the Chin Twins were back out on the streets of Beverly Hills, on neighborhood patrol.

"Keep your eyes peeled," Tom told Don. "I have a feeling in my bones about that robbery ring."

It had been widely reported that several homes had been robbed over the past few months. So far, the police hadn't been able to get any leads. They weren't even sure if any of the robberies were linked.

At that very moment, Trixie and Morty were picking the lock on the side door of Debbie's house. They were confident that the alarm system would not work because Trixie had activated a jamming device that was proven to outsmart wireless home security systems like Debbie's. She and Morty knew exactly what kind of security system Debbie had because Trixie had snapped a picture of it with her cell phone.

As soon as they managed to open the door, the alarm sounded—for less than a second.

"We're good to go," Morty said, opening drawers in the kitchen and stuffing Debbie's expensive silverware into one of the two large cloth bags he was holding. Less than a half hour later, all four of their bags were filled with everything—from silverware to jewelry to porcelain figurines and designer clothes, not to mention handbags, wallets, DVDs, CDs and anything else they thought would be valuable.

"Whatta haul," Trixie said, checking her watch. "Now let's get outta here."

They left the same way they came in, closing and locking the door behind them. At just that moment, the Chin Twins were walking across the street from Debbie's house.

"Whoa!" Don whispered urgently, pushing Tom behind a tree so they wouldn't be spotted. "We got 'em!"

As Trixie and Morty got into their van, the Chins ran halfway down the block to where their car was parked. They jumped in and pulled a U-turn so they could follow the crooks.

"We'd better call the cops," Tom said, pulling out his cell phone.

"No, wait!" Don urged. "First we have to follow them to their base. That's where all of the stolen goods will be hidden."

"Smart thinking, bro."

What the Chins didn't realize was that Trixie and Morty were already on to them. "We're being followed," Morty said, looking in the rearview mirror.

"Can you see who it is?"

Morty slowed down so the other vehicle would catch up to them and squinted. He blinked. "Unless I'm seein' double, it's a pair o' twins."

"The Chins!" Trixie said, remembering them from the audition.

"Yeah, they got chins," Morty said. "Pretty big chins, actually."

Trixie punched him in the arm. "No, idiot. That's their name—the Chin Twins."

"You're kidding me, right?"

"No," she insisted. "They're animal cops."

"Animal cops? Jeez, just what we need."

"What are we gonna do?" Trixie asked.

"I'll think of something. Okay, I thought of something." And he reached under his jacket and pulled out a revolver. It wasn't real—just a toy gun that he always brought along to scare people, in case someone caught them.

Trixie punched him in the arm again. "If they're cops, they're gonna know that's a fake."

"Except you said they're animal cops, not real cops."

The van pulled to a screeching stop in the alleyway behind Chateau Barkley. The Chins barely braked their car before crashing into it. And before they knew it, Morty was sticking a gun in their window. It was aimed straight at them.

"Get out wit' yer hands up, and don't make any quick moves!" he barked.

"Sir, you're breaking the law," Tom Chin declared.

"Thanks fer the news flash," Morty snorted. He waved the toy gun in their faces. "This gun look real enough to ya?"

"Y-yessir!" the Chins said in unison.

Morty grinned. "Then get outta that jalopy right now. *Go!*"

CHAPTER NINETEEN

Morty shoved the Chins into Chateau Barkley. Trixie found some rope and tied their hands behind their backs. Then she pointed at a large dog pen and ordered, "Get in."

"We're not going in there," Don Chin said defiantly.

Morty shoved the toy gun in his face. "Yes, you are."

The boarded dogs, each in their own private pen—except Neiman and Marcus, who were together—watched as the Chins did as they were told.

Morty reached into their pockets and found their cell phone. He took it with him as he left the pen, locking them in. He put the cell phone down on a table.

Neiman couldn't believe her eyes. "That's the Chin Twins," she barked. "From the audition."

"You're right," Marcus said. "The animal control officers."

"Something is definitely wrong here!"

"What are you talking about?" Max asked from his pen.

"They're holding those two officers against their will," Neiman explained. "I knew that woman was bad news from the moment I set eyes on her."

"What do you mean?" Lulu asked.

"She poisoned me at the movie audition so her precious Star could get the part."

As if on cue, the miniature poodle—who wasn't penned while Trixie and Morty were out robbing Debbie's house—ran up to Neiman and screamed, "You're a filthy liar!"

Fritzie spoke up. "I think *you're* a liar!"

"Please," Max pleaded, "everybody calm down."

Meanwhile, Morty was lugging four large bags into the room. He pulled an ornate silver candelabra out of one of them and set it on the floor. "That's gonna fetch a nice chunk o' change," he gloated.

"Does that look familiar to you?" Neiman asked her brother.

Trixie stuck her hand in another bag and pulled out a crystal pitcher. "This little number has gotta be worth a couple grand," she said, minus her French accent.

"Wait a minute," Marcus said. "Something's wrong here."

Trixie laughed raucously as she continued to pull items out of the bags. "Just wait'll that Debbie gets home and finds out we robbed her blind!"

"*What!*" Neiman cried out. "I knew that candelabra looked familiar!"

Marcus started jumping up and down. "What are we going to do?"

"They're nothing but lousy thieves!" Max screamed.

"And you're their partner in crime," Neiman snapped at the miniature poodle.

"So you got me," Sophie Smith snapped back. "What are you gonna do about it?"

Neiman stood on her hind legs, growling angrily. "Just wait'll I get my paws on you!"

Trixie pointed at the large pen and said, "What are we going to do with those two rubes?"

"Lemme think." Morty snapped his thick fingers. "Maybe they gotta suffer a horrible car accident."

"Or a horrible boating accident."

"Maybe they fall off the roof of a tall building."

"Or get squashed under a train."

"They could just disappear," Morty said, "never to be found again. That could definitely happen."

"We have friends in the police department," Tom Chin shouted. "They'll be looking for us anytime now."

"Nice try," Trixie said.

"No, seriously," Don Chin said. "We do have friends on the BHPD."

"Then your friends are gonna be real sad when they find out what happened to you," Morty chuckled.

Neiman turned to her brother and said, "We've got to do something."

Marcus was already thinking. "Remember how you slipped through our front gate? These bars aren't quite that far apart, but I think you can squeeze yourself through."

Neiman surveyed the bars and nodded. "What do I do after I get out?"

"Flip the latches on all of our pens," Fritzie suggested. "We'll run circles around them and create a diversion."

"We've got to free the Chins," Marcus said, "so they can call the police."

Neiman waited until the criminal trio stepped into a back room, where they were storing the stolen goods. It took some effort, but she managed to squeeze her body through the bars of the pen. Then she flipped the latch open, and Marcus came running out. Marcus flipped the latch on Max's pen while Neiman opened Lulu's pen, and then Lulu set Fritzie free.

Lulu watched as Marcus tried to jump up on the table where the cell phone was sitting. The short-legged bichon couldn't make it.

"No problem," the greyhound said, leaping easily onto the table and grabbing the cell phone in her mouth.

"Bring it here," Fritzie called as he opened the latch on the pen that the Chins were in.

"Good doggies," Tom Chin whispered, hoping they would have time to call the BHPD before Trixie and Morty caught on.

At that moment, Sophie trotted into the room and saw what was happening. She tried to run back into the other room to warn her accomplices, but Neiman sprinted in front of her and blocked her way.

"It's bichon against poodle," Neiman snarled.

"Get outta my way," Sophie snarled back.

Neiman stood her ground and wouldn't let Sophie get past her.

Max was chomping away at the ropes binding Don Chin, and Fritzie did likewise for Tom Chin. As Don pulled his hands free, Lulu opened her mouth and dropped the cell phone in them.

"What's all the ruckus?" Morty called out as he came running with a look of astonishment on his face.

Don punched numbers on his cell phone and reached police headquarters. "This is animal control officers Chin and Chin reporting a crime underway at"—he looked at the sign on the wall—"Chateau Barkley in Beverly Hills. Request immediate backup."

Morty came running at them with the fake gun. Fritzie scampered under his feet, and Morty went flying, crashing headfirst into one of the pens.

Trixie came screaming into the room, but Tom Chin was ready for her. He picked up the fallen gun and pointed it at her.

"You're under arrest for robbery and kidnapping, just for starters," he told her.

"That's a toy gun, you idiots," she said, rolling her eyes.

Tom looked at it. "You know," he told his brother, "she's right."

But by then, it didn't matter. Sirens were already wailing outside, and seconds later, the police arrived.

"Looks like you guys've nabbed yourselves some real hard cases," one of the officers said to the Chins as they led Trixie and Morty outside in handcuffs, with Sophie on a short leash.

Don Chin picked Neiman up and gave her a hug. "You were a real trooper that day at the audition," he told her. "That mean lady slipped you something that made you sick, didn't she? I thought so all along, and I'm going to tell that movie producer."

Tom bent down and group-hugged all the other dogs. "We couldn't have done it without you guys. You're the best!"

CHAPTER TWENTY

The police called Debbie and told her what had happened. Her only concern was that Neiman and Marcus were okay, and they assured her that they were doing just fine under the care and supervision of the Chins.

Two days later, when Debbie returned home, the Chins brought the pups to her, and Debbie tearfully hugged all of them—Neiman, Marcus, Tom, and Don. Later in the day, Debbie went to police headquarters, identified her stolen property, and got it all back.

Frank returned from Australia with some good news: his mother's condition had improved significantly, and the doctor claimed that she'd live to be a hundred. Frank was greatly relieved and happy that he had the opportunity to see her.

A few days after she'd been back, Debbie's phone rang. Donald Lawson—the producer of *It's a Dog's Life*—was on the line.

"I heard what happened at the audition and about the robbery," he told her. "I'm glad everyone's okay."

"Me too."

"I've already spoken with Artie Silver and told him I wanted to personally call you. Now that Margot Legrand's behind bars, Star won't be able to be in our film," Lawson explained. "So I'd like to hold a private audition for Neiman."

Debbie could hardly believe her ears. "You would?"

"Absolutely. Can you come in tomorrow?"

"Of course. See you then."

Debbie ran upstairs, where the pups were lounging in their Beverly Hills Hotel beds. "I've got the greatest news!" she cried out. "Neiman's getting another audition!"

Neiman sprang out of her bed and jumped up and down for joy. "This time, I can really show them what I can do."

"Does this mean we might be appearing in the film together?" Marcus asked.

"Count on it!" Neiman enthused.

Over the next two weeks, while Lois was still at camp, Debbie devoted most of her days to completing work on her new restaurant. She wanted Lois to be there for its grand opening, before she left for home. Debbie interviewed for the positions of chef, sous chef, and other kitchen staff, as well as food servers and a receptionist. Everything was coming together nicely.

The day finally came to pick Lois up at camp. Debbie got there early, parked the Rolls across the street from the entrance, and waited for Lois to appear. *I hope she's been having fun*, Debbie thought. They'd spoken on the phone a few times, but Debbie couldn't be sure until she had a chance to talk to her in person.

Debbie spotted Lois walking her way and waving. Not surprisingly, she was wearing her toque and ski jacket. Debbie got out of the Rolls and waved back, blinking her eyes. She was blinking because the three other girls who were walking with Lois were wearing the same outfit.

Lois made the introductions. "Aunt Debbie, this is Heather, Amber, and Ivy."

"Uh, hi, girls. Love your hats."

Heather said, "They're so cool, aren't they?"

"Where'd you get them?" Debbie asked.

"We ordered them online," Ivy said. "Lois has a great fashion sense, and we wanted to be like her."

"You're not hot in those ski jackets?" Debbie asked.

Amber shook her head. "We're not hot—we're cool!" And they all laughed.

Debbie noticed that some of the other girls were staring at them as if they're weren't "cool," but it didn't matter. Lois had made friends with girls who liked her for who she was. What more could you ask for?

The day before Lois was to leave, Debbie opened her restaurant. She had run an announcement in the *Beverly Hills Courier* newspaper that an exclusive new eatery was about to open, so a large crowd had gathered on the street.

Debbie's neighbor Goldie was among the first to arrive. "This is so exciting!" she shrieked. "I can't wait to eat here."

"We'll see," Debbie said with a sly smile.

Artie Silver was also among the crowd, as were Donald Lawson, Lawrence Fitzgerald, Janet the realtor, Dave the Pool Guy, and Justin. Frank was there, holding Neiman and Marcus. And, of course, the Chin Twins were in attendance.

The restaurant's sign was covered with a large canvas cloth. Debbie stepped under it and said, "I want to welcome everyone to my new restaurant. It's going to serve a very special clientele."

"I'm so proud of our mamma," Neiman told her brother.

"As we both are," Marcus replied.

With a flourish, Debbie pulled the string attached to the canvas cloth. It fell to the ground, revealing the name of the restaurant:

BISTRO LeMUTT
Exclusively for Dogs

The crowd erupted into loud applause and excited chatter.

"Welcome to Beverly Hills' first restaurant exclusively for dogs," Debbie announced proudly.

With that, the receptionist flung the doors open, revealing the ultra-chic interior that Debbie had designed.

Within the hour, as word spread throughout the streets of Beverly Hills, where dozens of shoppers were strolling with their dogs, Bistro LeMutt was filled to capacity.

Debbie's newest restaurant was an overnight sensation!

* * *

One year later, almost to the day, the world premiere of *It's a Dog's Life* was held in Hollywood. First to walk the red carpet was the male lead, a bull terrier named Wildfire. And right behind him was his romantic interest—Neiman. Not far behind her, among several other canine members of the cast, was Marcus.

"Oh, I just love that little man," Lawrence Fitzgerald, wearing a stunning purple tuxedo, commented.

Marcus heard Lawrence's heartfelt comment and winked at him. He felt exactly the same way.

Surrounded by all her new friends—as well as Lois and her parents, who had flown in for the occasion—Debbie was celebrating both the one-year anniversary of Bistro LeMutt and the acting debut of her two fabulous Beverly Hills bichons, Neiman and Marcus!

A successful restaurateur in her native Toronto and then in Scottsdale, Arizona, Debbie Bloy moved to Beverly Hills in 2000, along with her Bichons, Neiman and Marcus. In addition to writing books about the Beverly Hills Bichons, she runs an interior design consultancy for restaurants and homes. She spends her time in both Arizona and California, along with her newest animal companion, Star Bella.

CPSIA information can be obtained
at www.ICGtesting.com
Printed in the USA
FSHW02n2232060618
49064FS